DESERT
OF ICE

DESERT OF ICE

Life and Work in Antarctica

W. JOHN HACKWELL

Charles Scribner's Sons / New York

Collier Macmillan Canada • Toronto
Maxwell Macmillan International Publishing Group
New York • Oxford • Singapore • Sydney

To Morriss Kennedy,
my artist friend and mentor

Charles Scribner's Sons Books for Young Readers
Macmillan Publishing Company, 866 Third Avenue, New York, NY 10022

Collier Macmillan Canada, Inc., Suite 200, Don Mills, Ontario M3C 3N1

Printed in Singapore by Toppan Printing Co.
First Edition   10 9 8 7 6 5 4 3 2 1

Library of Congress Cataloging-in-Publication Data
Hackwell, W. John.
Desert of Ice: Life and Work in Antarctica / W. John Hackwell.—1st ed.
p.   cm.   Includes index.
Summary: Introduces the history and geography of Antarctica and describes life on an Antarctic base and the type of scientific research that is done there.
    ISBN 0-684-19085-0
1. Antarctic regions—Juvenile literature. [1. Antarctic regions.] I. Title.
G863.H33 1991   919.8'9—dc20   89-35002 CIP AC

Acknowledgments

The author wishes to acknowledge the valuable assistance of the following people and organizations: To my publishers, and especially my editor, Clare Costello, for her initial encouragement and guidance. To Bert Hunt of ABC Industries, Canberra, for his generous sponsorship. To the Australian Antarctic Division for making my Antarctic stay possible. To Captain Ewald Brune and the crew of *Icebird* for my safe journey. To Senator Graham Richardson and Jim Snow, MP, for my place in the Australian National Antarctic Research Expedition of 1989. To Dr. Desmond Lugg as expedition leader for his round-the-clock administration of my work and for later review of the manuscript. To Ian Hay as deputy voyage leader for providing me with computer access during the voyage. To Dr. Harry Black, Dr. John Gill, Utta Hosel, Rod Ledingham, and Eric Szworak for providing me with valuable transparencies. To Dr. Lawrence Johnson, John Bradfield, and Garth Varcoe for their help with the text. To Betty Milne and Windsor and Newton for a lifetime's supply of colored pencils. To my friends Tony Campbell and Jeff and Eleanor Watts, who would prefer that their generosity go unnoticed. And finally to Yvonne and my family for those marvelous words of encouragement during our many conversations via satellite while I was on the Antarctic continent.

Contents

Icebird's specially strengthened hull enables her to literally ride the floes and force huge slabs of ice to break off and float away as she slowly approaches Antarctica.

1

Assignment Antarctica

B igger than the United States and Mexico combined and representing ten percent of the earth's land mass, Antarctica has the greatest average altitude of any continent. Apart from a few coastal rocks and inland peaks, it is all solid ice two thousand meters (over six thousand feet) thick; eighty percent of the world's ice is there. But Antarctica is also a polar desert—no trees, no flowering plants, no rivers or white, sandy beaches. Its largest permanent inhabitant is a microorganism. All its ferns, freshwater fish, and reptiles are fossils. In the brief summer the sun rotates in the sky, barely descending at all, and in the long winter it never rises.

Antarctica is a place of frequent gales and blizzards and consistently records the world's lowest temperatures. Understandably, it is the only continent where no civilization has been established.

In 1773 Captain James Cook crossed the Antarctic Circle, although he saw no land. Since then many daring expe-

Today's expeditioners to the Antarctic come equipped with an array of scientific instruments rather than harpoons or guns. Here a scientist records the strength of the katabatic winds across the sea ice as an elephant seal surfaces nearby.

ditions have visited this matchless continent, but none could be called scientific in today's sense of the word. Most of the early voyages were associated with territorial claims.

Antarctica was seen as an infinite resource to be exploited, and this viewpoint led to the wanton slaughter of unique wildlife. Expeditions returned to their countries with huge hauls of sealskin and blubber oil. In the nineteenth century alone, elephant and fur seals were plundered almost to extinction. Female seals gathering on the sub-Antarctic islands to breed and give birth were slaughtered, leaving hundreds of thousands of young seals, or pups, to die. From whaling stations in the Antarctic Ocean the great whales were almost annihilated. Even today many colonies of rare marine mammals are struggling to recover.

Despite this atrocious beginning, Antarctica's recent history is marked with the exploits of men of great courage. While they too may have had little regard for the environment, they were daring explorers.

Today the world seems more enlightened, and harsh conditions have forced competing nations to work in a spirit of mutual concern.

In 1958 the twelve nations operating scientific research stations in Antarctica decided to work together by sharing scientific finds. On December 1, 1959, Argentina, Australia, Belgium, Chile, France, Japan, New Zealand, the United Kingdom, Norway, South Africa, the Union of Soviet Socialist Republics, and the United States signed a treaty in Washington guaranteeing that Antarctica would be used only for scientific purposes. The same treaty committed member nations to the free exchange of scientific information. Participants also agreed that no nuclear explosions would be set off on Antarctica and set up ways to monitor one another's compliance. Antarctica is, in effect, a demilitarized zone.

Since 1959 member nations have met regularly to formulate recommendations and to discuss their Antarctic priorities. Such priorities have included conservation, ways of minimizing human impact on the continent, the setting aside of areas for scientific research, and the development of an elaborate code of ethics. Member nations have also coordinated transportation and communications.

As a member of the Australian National Antarctic Research Expedition for 1989, I was excited by the prospect of crossing the world's largest glaciers and visiting remote islands to see indigenous wildlife. I soon came to realize that an expedition to the Antarctic was no afternoon nature walk.

Travel by ship would take fourteen days through the world's most treacherous and inhospitable oceans, where ten-meter (thirty-foot) waves and gale-force winds were common. Once on the continent I would confront other kinds of dangers. One Antarctic expeditioner who returned to base after several days of trekking discovered that the end of his thumb was missing. He had accidentally severed it some hours before and in the subzero temperatures had not felt any pain. The white-frosted thumb tip was still in his polar glove.

Most Antarctic expeditioners experience trauma of a far different kind. Scientists refer to it as behavioral adaptation. The term refers to the way humans react when confined for long periods in total isolation in a hostile environment. Such isolation often breeds dejection, despair, withdrawal, and strife. The earliest explorers certainly found it so. Some included straitjackets with their supplies.

Today's expeditions take both males and females, unlike the all-male groups of former years, and some say this has a positive effect on morale.

After medical tests and examinations had proved me

Preparation for an Antarctic journey by ship includes adequate training in fire safety and evacuation procedures. Here expedition members hurry to their lifeboat boarding point as part of that drill.

physically fit (anyone less than fit could become a liability), I was allocated a berth on the chartered West German ship *Icebird*. Designed and built for polar resupply, *Icebird* was to sail to Antarctica to resupply two Australian bases with cargo and fuel. It would carry an international observer under the treaty agreement and would take back scientists and support personnel who had wintered in Antarctica the preceding season.

High over the ocean a biologist bands an Antarctic fulmar that has come with a thousand others to nest on the cliffs of Kidson Island. Such ice-free sub-Antarctic islands are home to thousands of petrels and penguins during their breeding season.

Preparation for an Antarctic expedition must be thorough. Scientific teams calculate their laboratory requirements months in advance. If they will be working in the field rather than confined to a base, they must advise organizers of their need for surface vehicles and field huts and estimate the number of helicopter hours they will require.

During every Antarctic summer, treaty nations send scientists to Antarctica to carry out a wide range of investigations. Some require international cooperation to succeed. It is not uncommon, for instance, for the United States to support as many as three hundred scientific personnel under the direction of the National Science Foundation.

My expedition to Antarctica was typical of most in that it included biologists, meteorologists, geochemists, and geologists, as well as a contingent of television news and film crews to record events of public interest. There were also the support and logistics personnel whose job it is to provide backup to the fieldwork.

The expedition's departure point was Hobart, Australia. I joined other expeditioners there for a briefing, became acquainted with the voyage leader and scientific personnel, and collected my polar clothing from the Australian Antarctic Division.

Predeparture briefings are designed primarily to instill confidence and give first-time travelers a sense of well-being.

Safety has a high priority for Antarctic expeditioners. A fall into the icy Southern Ocean, as they often call the Antarctic Ocean, can result in death within minutes even if the victim is rescued. Hypothermia, or abnormally low body temperature, may cause death both in the water and on land. One traveler who was wearing only summer clothing walked out of a heated building on an Antarctic base, encountered an unexpected blizzard, fell and broke his ankle, became disoriented, and was fortunately rescued just a few steps from safety. The result could have been far different.

With my briefing concluded and personal baggage loaded into our waiting car, the expedition party drove to the *Icebird* at Hobart dock. One expeditioner, already contemplating polar privation, commented that our experience was the earthly equivalent of a space-shuttle departure.

2

Sailing South

Expeditions to Antarctica fall broadly into two categories. Government-sponsored scientific undertakings are usually long-term projects requiring international cooperation. Then there are the private adventures, which some would say are the more imaginative and creative. Often they are attempts to relive the pioneer expeditions. While today's privately sponsored expeditions do undertake some scientific investigations, critics view them as fanciful or even ill conceived. There is no doubt that they are directed by people with entrepreneurial and sailing skills, and the directors vigorously claim to be independent, but they sometimes need the assistance of foreign governments when they arrive in Antarctic waters. Such adventurers often receive spectacular media coverage that arouses public support for their much-debated bravery.

My journey to Antarctica was government sponsored,

but we hoped it would have all the spirit of a true adventure without undue risk to the expeditioners!

For one hour prior to departure, immigration officials searched *Icebird* for stowaways. I couldn't imagine anyone stowing away to visit the coldest, driest, windiest, most impenetrable and remote continent on this planet.

Expeditioners gathered at portside to cheer and wave; some would not see their families and friends again for more than a year.

There are significant dangers for any Antarctic supply ship. Rows of drums filled with explosive chemicals stand tied to the forward deck, making fire safety a matter of utmost importance to captain and crew. When a supply ship is a thousand nautical miles from any land, the last thing the operation needs is a fire.

As *Icebird* glided slowly down the Derwent River toward the open sea, the ship's safety officer assembled all expeditioners to familiarize them with lifeboat and evacuation procedures. Everyone was required to assemble in full polar dress in preparation for such an emergency. When the routine was completed we were reminded that no safety drill would be unannounced. If the ship's sirens sounded without prior warning it should be taken as a genuine emergency and everyone should dress appropriately and assemble beside the appointed lifeboat.

Out on the decks expeditioners began the exciting process of becoming acquainted. I met an American professor of philosophy who was journeying to Antarctica to pursue an interest in environmental ethics. There was an oceanographer and an English geology student whose fieldwork would take him into some of the most scenic regions of the continent. I met a fellow artist, a wildlife photographer, and a photojournalist from Austria, as well as a contingent of

A journey to the Antarctic may be the realization of a lifetime's dream. Here the families of scientists gather at portside as *Icebird* prepares for departure.

politicians, reporters, and various support staff.

Polar ships, especially icebreakers, have unique capabilities. Japan, Russia, and the United States all send icebreakers to Antarctic waters. These powerful vessels are capable of smashing their way through vast ice floes two or three meters (six to ten feet) thick and are often used in support of smaller ships during oceanic research.

Whatever a ship's capability, endurance is perhaps the most important feature, since it may take more than ten days to reach Antarctica only to discover that pack ice, or frozen salt water, has extended the continent by as much as two hundred kilometers (over one hundred twenty miles). In these adverse conditions small ketches or yachts could easily be crushed as enormous pressure builds between ice floes. If a ship encounters extensive pack ice, fuel stocks may be required to last for several months.

Antarctic ships need deep-sea trawl and hydrographic winches to assist with scientific experiments. They also need cranes that are capable of maneuvering helicopters and containers, often in arduous circumstances.

Scuba gear, holding tanks, and zodiacs or similar landing craft with sea-land capability are essential because ships may have to anchor some distance from Antarctic bases. Precision depth recorders, satellite communications, and navigational receivers—radio, telephone, and, of most importance, radar—are all standard requirements for such polar vessels.

When one travels day after day in five-meter (fifteen-foot) swells, one acquires a sense of the vastness and unforgiving spirit of the Antarctic Ocean. Not even the occasional sighting of a wandering albatross is any indication that land is nearby, since these giant birds can fly for two or three years without touching down on land. Occasionally they will swoop

A ten-day journey on a supply vessel to the Antarctic can result in boredom, but the first sighting of a rare whale or a seabird generally changes all that!

It is hard to imagine that penguins on some sub-Antarctic islands were virtually exterminated by nineteenth-century whaling crews. As *Icebird* pauses at the ice edge, Adélie penguins delight us by their tameness and almost human social behavior.

in low at the stern of the ship and glide away into the distance, never to be seen again.

It is the icebergs, however, that silently announce to the visitor that something unimaginable is ahead. These monumental, seemingly motionless giants of the Southern Ocean are unrivaled anywhere in the world.

It is not uncommon to see several flat-topped, or tabular, bergs perhaps twenty kilometers (twelve and a half miles) in length, or even forty kilometers (twenty-five miles). The blue horizontal banding—like growth rings on a giant tree—indicates the number of years an iceberg has been forming on Antarctica's plateau.

Glacier bergs are illuminated from inside in tones of azure blue and deep green. When *Icebird* entered their shadow I wanted to reach out and touch their dazzling white, knifelike edges and deep crevasses. As we drew even closer we could see huge caves and spurs on their waterlines. These jaggered giants seemed to protrude one hundred meters (over three hundred feet) into the sky, and at times we were surrounded by them!

After several more days in very rough seas we were jolted awake as the ship encountered pack ice for the first time. As the vessel plowed its way through the ice, penguins scrambled for the safety of distant floes. Antarctica was now very close!

The voyage leader reminded us again of our obligations to the strange and beautiful world just ahead. We would be aliens in this land, perhaps intruders, and we would have to proceed with good intentions. We were not to walk on fragile mosses and close-textured lichens, so slow to grow that our footprints would still be there in ten years' time. We were not to remove fossils or minerals or disturb the seals and penguins, especially when the penguins were nesting, as they might have a twenty- or thirty-kilometer (fifteen-mile) walk to the ocean to feed in order to replenish the energy they would lose when disturbed.

Nothing decomposes or deteriorates in the Antarctic—it just freezes—and field expeditioners must collect all litter and human waste and return it to the base to be burned. This is especially true of flesh food scraps. Nothing is to be thrown to the wildlife, as this may introduce new viruses into their systems.

After twenty-five hundred nautical miles *Icebird* was at last breaking ice only thirty-five kilometers (over twenty miles) off the continent. Tomorrow at eight we would be flown by helicopter to undertake our various assignments. We were experiencing constant daylight now, and almost everyone on the ship had lost interest in sleep. With polar clothing on and cameras in place, we were ready for our first steps on Antarctica.

From where I stood on the flying bridge it seemed that we were very near our anchorage, but visibility in the Antarctic is deceptive. The air is so free of dust particles and moisture that features perhaps thirty kilometers (twenty miles) away have the clarity and definition of a house across the street.

Icebird has a specially shaped, full double hull to provide maximum protection from ice damage. This morning nearly all the passengers were crammed onto the bridge, watching as she rode the pack ice and smashed it into a turbulent, heaving mess. After an hour or so of such maneuvering, the ship's captain was airlifted by helicopter to undertake an ice reconnaissance flight while a second helicopter transferred the voyage leader and other personnel to Australia's Davis Station. Before long it seemed that the air was filled with the thrashing of helicopters as one after the other airlifted mail and fresh fruit and vegetables to a very eager winter party ashore.

Meanwhile the ship's rotating electrohydraulic cranes hoisted polar barges and other landing craft over the side and began loading them with crates of scientific equipment, pre-fabricated building modules, vehicles, and a great variety of supplies. These supplies were lashed to the barges and ferried to the base. Very soon the barges would return with containerized waste materials in order to keep Antarctica clean.

Often polar supply ships are long delayed, even when they arrive at an Antarctic ice wharf. Sudden blizzards,

With weather so unpredictable, crews work in continuous shifts until the resupply is completed. If sea ice prevents direct entry to a harbor, specially equipped barges are used to transport cargo to the Antarctic base.

Here at Australia's Mawson station, the terrain is so rocky and irregular that electrical cables and water pipes are fitted to a very accessible grid.

heavy ice, or unexpected breakdowns can change a three-day project into one that takes three or more weeks.

By the time my name was called to transfer ashore I had already climbed into my heavy polar clothing. Nothing had prepared me for the moment when the chopper looped away from the ship, dipped, then banked. Laid out below me was an endless display of neatly broken pack ice looking in every way like a giant marble pavement. Behind me as far as the eye could see were hundreds of icebergs. In the foreground to the right was an old berg grounded on the continental shelf, its toothed and notched form suggesting it had been struggling for several years in that very position.

Just then I saw a couple of islands wedged all around in thick blue ice, looking like chunky decorations on a gigantic wedding cake. Up ahead again I could see the white Antarctic plateau: mile upon mile of gleaming white ice. In fact, it was brighter than white; it was yellow-white. When I momentarily closed my eyes tight, they filled with the strongest aqua blue and red-purple I have ever experienced, the complementaries of yellow-white.

Now in the foreground I had my first view of an Antarctic base. I could see a rocky, ice-free promontory with a concentration of red, green, and blue buildings, color coded for safety. There were aerials, wires, communications towers, radar domes, excavations, piles of iron frames, fuel drums, and still more towers.

As the chopper circled I caught glimpses of containers and crates and empty gas bottles and row upon row of shiny pipes linking the various buildings. I learned later that these were sewage and water pipes kept above ground for ease of repair during winter blizzards. Before I could take it all in we had landed.

3

Life on an Antarctic Base

Antarctic stations must be functional and fire safe. Because surface air temperatures are very low, the air carries little moisture and old timber buildings can easily ignite.

The location and design of buildings must take into account the unyielding and often violent blizzards that force sleet as fine as talc to pile up and bury them. While a blizzard is blowing it may take an expeditioner twenty minutes to negotiate a distance that normally takes only five.

One of the key persons on an Antarctic base is the administrative director, or station leader, who is responsible for the day-to-day running of the station and need not have scientific training. Station leaders are required to coordinate staff orientation, field training, and precision fire drills and to assign the various personnel and organize supplies. Such leaders must be able to delegate responsibility, communicate well, and act decisively in a crisis. In isolated communities, the leader must also be a caring and sensitive counselor. Big-

Many nations operate small field bases in scientifically important areas. At Australia's Law base, flags on the hut welcome Russian and Chinese personnel also here.

Dog sledding and ice yachting are two of the more vigorous outdoor pursuits available to Antarctic expeditioners.

ger bases such as America's McMurdo have chaplains to carry out the latter role.

Recreational life on an Antarctic base can include such indoor activities as basketball, music, photography, art, and perhaps ice sculpture, while outdoor sports and leisure interests can be somewhat more innovative. Dog sledding, cross-country skiing, even ice golf and yachting have taken place here. With the right wind an ice yacht can race across the sea ice at forty kilometers (twenty-five miles) an hour!

Expeditioners who spend a year on the continent speak in awed tones of Antarctica's winter appearance and moods. They believe that the ultimate Antarctic experience is to cross the icy plateau in midwinter.

For such traverses, as they are called, huge bulldozers tow laboratories and accommodation cabins and sleds of fuel and food supplies to support scientific personnel for several months. Some even take husky teams to provide flexibility and perhaps a nostalgic link with the past.

When a winter traverse has been pinned down for several days in a severe blizzard, the huskies provide essential team-support.

Life on an Antarctic station has its compensations. Here scientists take a recreational drive around a high plateau where the ice is 4,000 meters (2½ miles) thick.

Whatever the scientific reason for traversing, the weather is often cruel and always unpredictable. Invariably it determines one's success and the time one can spend in the field.

Antarctica's icy interior forces traverse teams to take much longer than normal to perform everyday tasks. To obtain a cup of water, for example, snow or ice must first be heated and then cooled, but the result is the purest water in the world. There are no luxuries on a traverse, and while food may be nutritious it often lacks variety. But the pioneers had it much harder. Their food rations were often just ship biscuits, penguin eggs, and seal meat.

During violent blizzards, biting winds penetrate heavy clothing and cause energy loss; if the expeditioner is too active, perspiration increases, the level of body fluids drops, and life can be quite miserable. Such blizzards cause frozen snow to form mile after mile of wrinkled and scalloped ice waves called sastrugi. These hardened surfaces place extra strain on steel linkages and cut dogs' feet, making progress impossible.

But all scientific expeditioners to Antarctica say that it is not difficult to endure a cold face or to sleep a night or two on a frozen floor. The climate is the easiest to adjust to. Enduring enforced hibernation in a small, crowded room or tent—eating, resting, watching, waiting, cloistered day after day with the same few people—this is Antarctica's greatest test! Then again, when the blizzard subsides, the scenery is majestic. Everyone in Antarctica has something important to do. It is this sense of purpose, of scientific discovery and achievement, that makes it all worthwhile.

4

Scientific Research

If the nineteenth century was characterized by competitive exploitation, the latter half of this century will be remembered as a time of cooperative science. Scientists the world over agree that Antarctic information plays a pivotal role in understanding global phenomena. They come here from many nations seeking to understand the nature and evolution of Antarctica's life forms and environment.

Antarctic waters, for example, are a vital component of our overall understanding of the world's oceans. Scientists have spent several decades studying the sea floor; the spreading of the global sea floor is described as the earth's primary geophysical process.

Other scientists study the Antarctic bottom water, an icy, dense body of water that sinks and spreads globally. They also study climatic cycles, variations of current, and the way sediments are transported from the continental shelf to the ocean floor.

This glaciologist uses a sophisticated radio-echo sounding device to measure the movements of ice.

Other oceanographers concentrate on the ice edge, which in the spring covers some twenty million square kilometers (nearly eight million square miles), an area greater than the whole of the Antarctic continent. When this ice breaks up and retreats, algae bloom and become an important feeding area for marine mammals and birds. Scientists place dye in the plankton to observe and record the feeding patterns of these creatures.

One important study is that of the Antarctic krill, a shrimplike crustacean that forms the basis of the Southern Ocean food chain. Whales alone devour hundreds of thousands of tons of krill each year. Biologists try to learn how the krill develops, feeds, and spawns, and how mammals and birds go about feeding on it.

Biologists also study seals to observe the relationship between mothers and pups, the overtures of the males, and the mating ritual. Seals are captured and weighed, and monitors are attached to their dorsal area to measure their heartbeat, their swimming speed, and the depth of their dive. In this way scientists hope to better understand their numbers and survival rates.

One morning I flew with two ornithologists to Kidson Island, about eighteen kilometers (ten miles) off the continent, to observe a colony of Antarctic fulmars nesting. As we approached this windswept and barren island, cape petrels and other birds flew from almost every conceivable nook and cranny. As the sky filled with birds I felt for a horrible moment like a trespasser.

But once we were on the ground it was a different story. When we had counted and ringed the fulmars I went to investigate a colony of Adélie penguins and managed to spend a couple of hours alone amid a cacophony of braying birds and their bleeping chicks. I had observed from books that the best pictures of penguins were taken with the camera held very close to the ground, so I decided to lie facedown in the middle of this orange-stained rookery and allow these curious and lovable creatures to come to me.

As I lay there, one intensely busy bird hurried about gathering small pebbles in his beak and placed them in an orderly manner about his mate, even though their chicks were almost fully grown. I couldn't help but wonder about a creation that commands these absorbing creatures to multiply in this place!

Here biologists bag a dead emperor penguin as other birds stand motionless nearby. Colonies of the majestic emperors spend the entire winter at these traditional nursery sites.

A meteorologist launches a hydrogen balloon that has been fitted with instruments for measuring specific aspects of Antarctica's climate.

One of the more fascinating studies going on in Antarctica involves the emperor penguins. Scientists attach monitors to these birds to measure their swimming and feeding habits and to record the depth of their dive. Emperors have been recorded diving more than three hundred meters (nearly one thousand feet) below the ocean's surface.

Glaciologists study the continental ice shelf and surrounding sea ice to learn the physical properties of the ice, its internal stability, and the dynamics of its movement. They study the glaciers themselves, the debris they deposit, and the movement of the ice streams they create, in the hope of predicting what these glaciers will do in the future.

Glaciologists are also interested in world climates of the past. They use seismic and radio-echo sounding devices and undertake deep ice-core drilling to observe large-scale changes over the past ten thousand years. When this data is combined with information from Alaska, Greenland, and China, global climates can be described more accurately.

Since Antarctica is the major cooling center for our planet, meteorologists study its weather patterns to understand how they influence global climates. Some stations launch hydrogen balloons equipped with instruments for measuring wind temperature, carbon dioxide levels, surface ozone, atmospheric moisture, and air pressure. Ground-based radar tracks these balloons until they burst in the upper atmosphere.

Other instruments monitor radiation and record the chemical composition of the atmosphere. Field researchers set up miniature weather stations to provide forecasters with regular data via satellite.

Scientists also study Antarctica's unique katabatic winds—chilled, dense bodies of air driven off the polar plateau, not by atmosphere or rotation, but by gravity. Data

Since the majority of scientific undertakings are attempted in a brief three-month period, helicopters are used extensively to support field teams in remote locations.

on seasonal changes are collected and analyzed to determine the effect of the winds on local climate.

The Antarctic is also an ideal platform from which to probe the earth's upper atmosphere. Scientists study various optical phenomena and magnetic pulsations to see their effects on radio waves.

Terrestrial biologists study the ecology of Antarctic lakes to learn how various forms of marine life relate to one another. Some scientists specialize in benthic, or bottom-dwelling, algae to observe how they adapt in very dark waters. Others concentrate on the effects of glacial meltwater as it pours into these lakes. Underwater sensors read changing oxygen levels and their effects on organisms.

Geological projects include mapping and structural analysis, surveys of earth tremors, and the study of volcanic deposits to learn how they react with water during eruption.

Organic geochemical studies are essential to understanding crude oils. Certain bacteria preceded petroleum-source rocks, coals, and oil shales; scientists compare these chemical structures in Antarctica with those produced by similar bacteria in different environments.

Medical scientists are also working in Antarctica to study the impact of the environment on humans. They study the effects of stress and depression of the immune system of the staff who remain in Antarctica for extended periods, as well as the effects of diet and nutrition on health.

Every summer, scientists come from countries all over the world with projects too numerous to mention. When they return home it may take months, even years, to fully analyze and complete their work.

5

The Future of Antarctica

Every expeditioner who visits Antarctica comes away with lasting impressions of an amazing and unique world—perhaps of ten-story-high sculptured icebergs silhouetted against a blackened sky, or of minke or killer whales cruising silently in their shadows. They may be the memories of a blue frozen and burnished lake with a surface so hard that metal-tracked vehicles leave no trace.

My own impressions are of very personal encounters with the wildlife. I remember watching from the rocks as a bloodred and battered Adélie penguin clambered and toothed its way to the rookery. Obviously it had been savaged by a leopard seal. I watched with a sense of helplessness as it stood with its beak tucked under its flipper, shivering and tortured, awaiting an untimely death.

I remember trekking in the Masson ranges perhaps thirty kilometers (eighteen miles) from the ocean and finding

As two expeditioners stroll across the ice, a lone leopard seal acknowledges their presence.

the bleached and mummified bodies of a lone seal and an emperor penguin. Apparently they had wandered, disoriented, in this unknown place and eventually died from lack of energy and food. As I inspected the powerful crampons on the feet of the majestic penguin I wondered if it had died last year or three hundred years ago.

As our vessel glided away from that icy world I had already forgotten the offensive stench of the penguin rookeries. I watched from the bow as these incredible swimmers porpoised through the water to avoid being crushed by the oncoming ship. I watched in awe as one after the other made an incredible two-point, jet-propelled landing on nearby floating ice. I wanted to cheer when they reached the safety of the floes.

My thoughts turned to present dangers. Whaling and sealing have been phased out, but the emerging krill-harvesting industry could well create an imbalance in this finely tuned ecosystem.

Because of its remoteness, severity of climate, and thick ice cover, the Antarctic continent seems unlikely to be exploited for minerals, but considering the high rate of depletion of the world's crude-oil reserves and the level of scientific investment here, the possibility cannot be overlooked.

We can only hope that the present era of scientific cooperation will not be replaced by the commercial rivalry of greedy governments.

Some people want to see the "spoils" of Antarctica— whether offshore oil, krill, or even the bagging and selling of icebergs for fresh water—divided among the nations involved in its exploration.

Others would like the United Nations to take over the management and distribution of Antarctica's resources to en-

An Adélie chick reaches in and snatches a morsel of food from the bill of the parent bird. Any decision about the future of Antarctica must surely recognize that the needs of nonhuman visitors such as these come first.

sure that they are divided evenly. Still others, pointing to the sensitive issues of ozone depletion and worldwide pollution, suggest that Antarctica should be left alone altogether and turned into a world heritage or wilderness park. Many expeditioners dedicate their work to this end.

Antarctica is undoubtedly the continent least affected by industrialized society. As a relatively unpolluted wonderland it is unique and must be preserved for future generations, who may well judge us by the degree of moral sensibility and respect we showed for this great, icy desert.

Index

Index